Why Grizzly Bears Walk On All Fours

A Mount Shasta Native American Story

A Joaquin Miller Story
retold by LINDA WALLACE

Illustrations by Kathleen Langford

Why Grizzly Bears Walk on All Fours
©2013 L. J. L. Publishing 2013

Published by L. J. L. Publishing Co.
Printed by Create Space

International Standard Book Number: 978-1-893923-27-0

Copyright ©2013
All rights reserved, including the right of
reproduction in whole or in part in any form.

Why Grizzly Bears Walk on All Fours by Linda Wallace
Illustrated by Kathleen Langford
Book design by Tracy Tuttle

Native American legends are stories told through generations.
Some are based on fact or fiction, and may have changed after years of retelling.

This story presents an early Native American explanation of creation in the
Mount Shasta region of Northern California.

This story is retold and adapted by Linda Wallace, from Joaquin Miller's,
"Unwritten History: Life Amongst the Modocs," American Publishing Company, 1874.

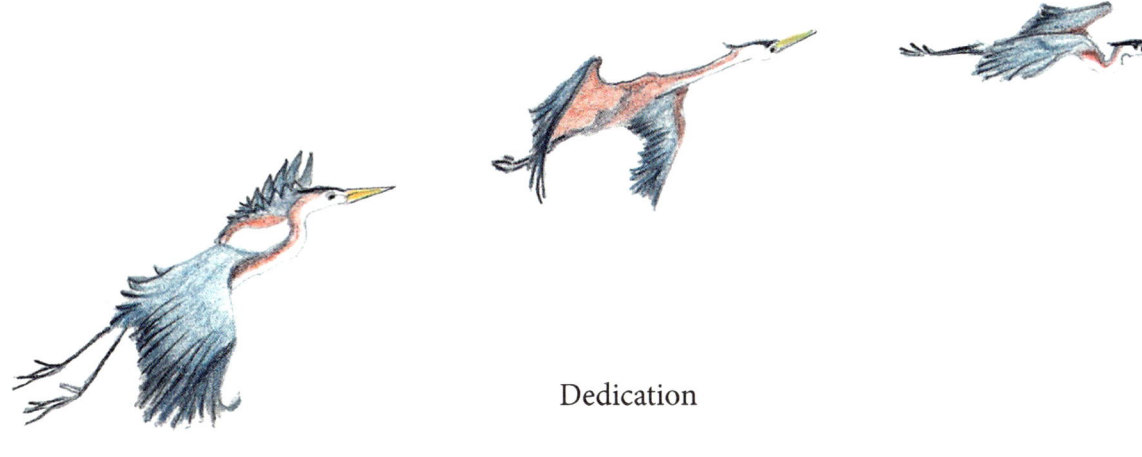

Dedication

This book is dedicated to the Native American tribes, such as the Shasta, Wintu, Modoc, Pit River, Hat Creek, Karuk, Hupa, and others who frequented the Mount Shasta area for centuries. These tribes were strong, beautiful, and proud people who revered the land that nourished them. Their history is found within and from them, in books, or at museums in our area. Their descendants today carry their knowledge and traditions. This creation myth is thought to have come from the Shasta tribe.

It is dedicated to Joaquin Miller for recording stories we all can enjoy today. "Why Grizzly Bears Walk On All Fours" is one among many.

Kathleen and I dedicate it to children everywhere. All delight in learning, growing, and becoming educated, when stimulated with appropriate material. That is why this book has come to fruition. May you delight in its pathways into the natural World!

It is also dedicated to our families who helped us in the journey of publishing. We are hopeful our grandchildren, nieces and nephews, adults and friends, and our descendants, will enjoy this fictional story, our gift to you.

"The Indians with whom I once lived in the Californian Sierras held the grizzly bear in great respect and veneration... He venerated the grizzly bear as his paternal ancestor."

—Joaquin Miller,
from the The Great Grizzly Bear (Ursus Ferox.)

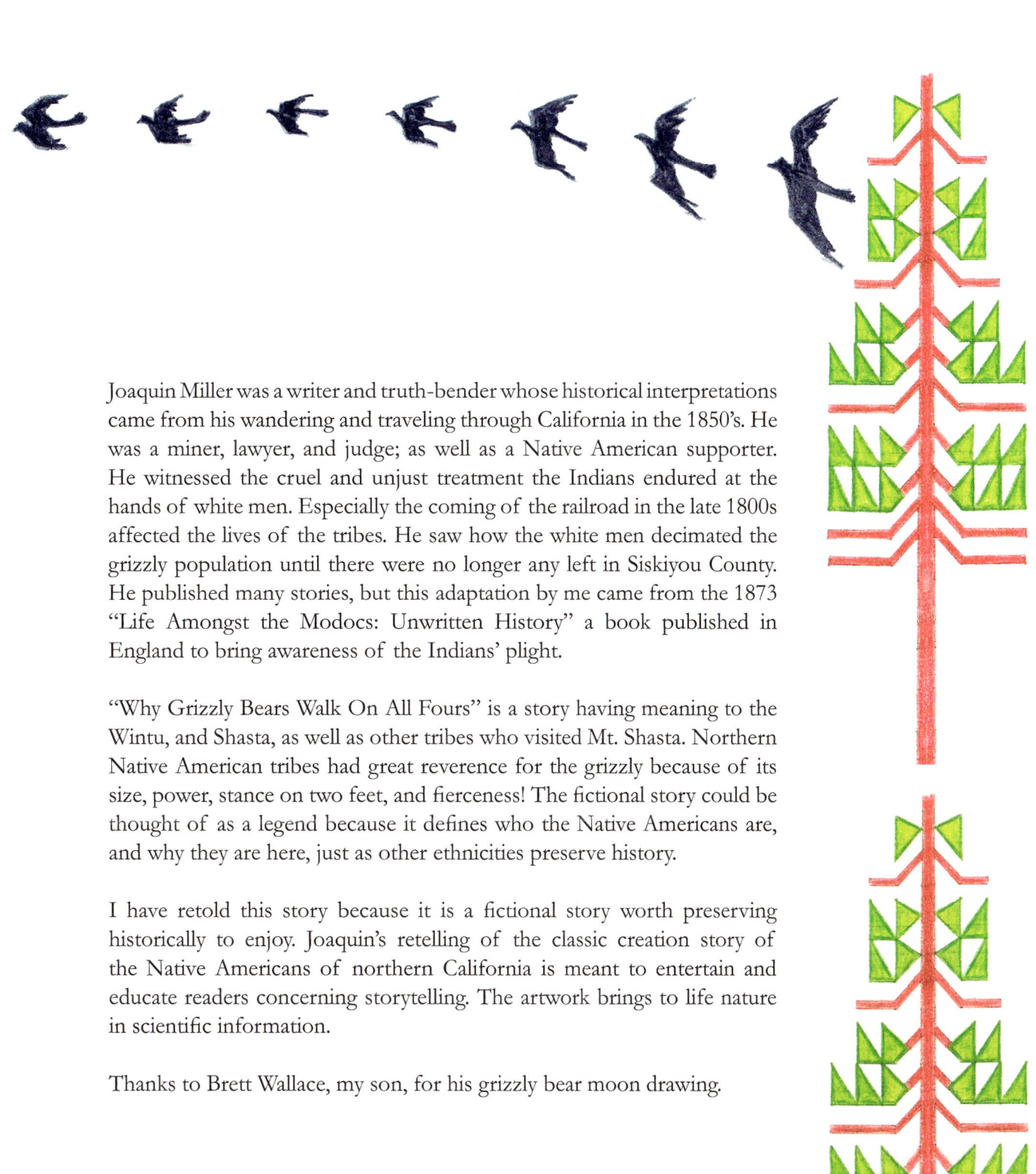

Joaquin Miller was a writer and truth-bender whose historical interpretations came from his wandering and traveling through California in the 1850's. He was a miner, lawyer, and judge; as well as a Native American supporter. He witnessed the cruel and unjust treatment the Indians endured at the hands of white men. Especially the coming of the railroad in the late 1800s affected the lives of the tribes. He saw how the white men decimated the grizzly population until there were no longer any left in Siskiyou County. He published many stories, but this adaptation by me came from the 1873 "Life Amongst the Modocs: Unwritten History" a book published in England to bring awareness of the Indians' plight.

"Why Grizzly Bears Walk On All Fours" is a story having meaning to the Wintu, and Shasta, as well as other tribes who visited Mt. Shasta. Northern Native American tribes had great reverence for the grizzly because of its size, power, stance on two feet, and fierceness! The fictional story could be thought of as a legend because it defines who the Native Americans are, and why they are here, just as other ethnicities preserve history.

I have retold this story because it is a fictional story worth preserving historically to enjoy. Joaquin's retelling of the classic creation story of the Native Americans of northern California is meant to entertain and educate readers concerning storytelling. The artwork brings to life nature in scientific information.

Thanks to Brett Wallace, my son, for his grizzly bear moon drawing.

Many moons ago, a great storm came to the summit of Mount Shasta. The white peak, piercing the sky, was home to the Great Spirit and his family. His lodge was inside the mountain.

The Great Spirit spoke to his youngest and fairest daughter, "Climb to the hole in the top of this mountain. Speak to the storm coming from the sea. Tell it to be gentle, or it will blow the mountain over."

"Do this hastily," said the Great Spirit. "Do not put your head out, lest the wind catch your hair and blow you away! Thrust out your long, red arm and make a sign. Speak softly to the storm to calm it."

The Indian Princess hastened to the top of the lodge to do as she was told. Having never seen the ocean where the wind was born, she dared to lift her head out of the hole in the mountain. Lo! The storm caught her long red hair . . . and lifted her out.

Down, down the mountain she tumbled. She could not fix her feet in the hard, smooth ice and snow. On and on she tumbled past the white firs below the snow rim.

Now the Grizzly Bear Tribe possessed all the woods and land to the sea. They were very numerous and very, very powerful. The bears walked upright on two legs. They were more human than beast. They lived in caves and had sharp claws. The tribe used clubs to fight instead of using their teeth and claws.

A family of grizzlies lived close to the snow line. When Old Father Grizzly went hunting each day he would return carrying his club in one hand and an elk over his shoulder.

By chance, he noticed a small creature with red skin and red hair trailing in the snow. The creature was crouched beneath a fir bush, shivering, cold, terrified of the huge beast!

Old Father Grizzly didn't know what to make of her. He took her to Old Mother Grizzly who was learned in all things.

"This child belongs to the Great Spirit," roared Mother Grizzly. "We will not tell him she is with us."

Mother Grizzly always got her way. "Leave this child with me. I will raise her with the other children. Do not say anything about her to anyone."

Each day Old Father Grizzly went out to hunt food for his family. Before long the children were grown.

"Our oldest son is quite grown up. He needs a wife," said Mother Grizzly. "Let him take the little red creature you found in the snow, as his wife."

Old Father Grizzly kissed her and said, "You are very wise!" Raising his club to his shoulder, he went to hunt for meat for the marriage feast.

The Grizzly Bear's Son and the Indian Princess were married. They were very happy. Many children were born to them. Being part of the Great Spirit and part of the Grizzly Bear Tribe, the children did not look like either of their parents.

Thus, the Redman was created.
These children were the first Native Americans.

All the Grizzly Bear Tribe throughout the giant forest, even down to the sea, were very proud and kind to the Redmen. United in strength and power, they built a wigwam close to the Great Spirit's lodge for the Princess. This was known as "Little Mount Shasta" or Shastina.

Many years passed. Old Mother Grizzly grew very old. She became ill and was sure to die. Fear filled her very being, for the wrong she had done to the Great Spirit. She knew she could not rest, and must speak to the Great Spirit. The Indian Princess, his long-lost treasure, had to be returned.

"I must ask for his forgiveness," she thought.

Mother Grizzly gathered together all the Grizzly Bear Tribe at the new magnificent lodge built for the Princess and her children.

She sent her eldest grandson up the summit of Mount Shasta in a cloud to speak to the Great Spirit. "You will find your long-lost daughter at Shastina, the new lodge lower on the mountain," spoke the grandson to the Great Spirit.

The Great Spirit was glad of this news. He ran down the south side of the mountain so fast and strong, the snow melted off in places, just as it remains today.

The Grizzly Bear Tribe, numbering in the thousands, went out to greet the Great Spirit. As he approached, they stood apart in two great lines, carrying clubs under their arms. He passed through the lines of bears, to his daughter who sat inside the new lodge with her children.

Great Spirit was very angry. The Grizzly Bear tribe, whom he had created, had betrayed him. "Those do not look like my daughter's children. You have created a new race!" roared the Great Spirit.

"Please forgive me, Great Spirit," she pleaded.

At that moment she lay very still. No longer could she take a breath. Then Old Mother Grizzly entered the flower trail to the West. Instantly the entire Grizzly Bear Tribe set up a dreadful howl!

16

The Great Spirit took his daughter. He raised his hand to leave and said, "You grizzlies must hold your tongues. Get down on your hands and haunches. You will remain this way forever!"

As he turned to look, all the bears were on all fours.

He closed the door to the lodge. All the Redmen's children went out into the world, never to return to the snow-covered mountain again.

As proof of this story, all the Grizzly Bear Tribe can no longer rise up or use their clubs. They are cursed to walk on all fours, much like other beasts. When they must fight, the Great Spirit has granted them permission to stand up and fight with their fists, as men do.

That is why the Native Americans of Mount Shasta will never kill or interfere in any way with the grizzlies. Whenever one of their numbers is killed by one of the kingly beasts of the forest, he is burned on the spot. All who pass that way for years will cast a stone on the place, until a great pile is thrown up.

Today there are no grizzlies on Mount Shasta. The grizzly bear once walked upright like men, with scarcely any tail. Their arms were shorter than their legs. They were more like men, than any other animal!

Plant Identifications & Uses

The following information is taken in part from Verne Frederick Ray's Primitive Pragmatists: The Modoc Indians of Northern California. University of Washington Press. 1963.

Lodgepole Pine
(Pinus contorta)

Seeds and cambium bark layer were used for food. Resin was used as eye medicine or chewed to relieve mouth and throat soreness.

Page 2

Incense Cedar
(Calocedrus decurrens)

Wood was used for fire drill hearths. Resin was chewed for colds, coughs, and for sore throats. The trunks were used for making boats.

Page 3

Pacific Yew
(Taxus brevifolia)

Wood from this tree was used to make bows, spears, and boat paddles.

Page 4

Western Juniper (Juniperus occidentalis)

Juniper was used for basket fibers and bows. For colds and coughs the smoke was inhaled or an infusion was made from leaves. Smoke was also inhaled for sore throats. An infusion of leaves or berries was used to treat urinary problems.

Page 5

Sugar Pine
(Pinus lambertiana)

Nuts of the sugar pine trees were used for food and beads. Resin was used to treat wounds and sores.

Page 6

White Fir
(Abies concolor)

Dye was made from the bark. Resin was chewed for sore throat. Resin was also used on wounds and sores. The trunks of the white fir were used to make boats.

Page 7

Mountain Mahogany
(Cercocarpus ledifolius)

Mountain mahogany was used for products requiring a dense, hard wood.

Page 8

Desert Parsley
(Lomatium macrocarpum)

The root of the desert parsley was used for food.

Page 9

Blue Camas
(Camassia quamash)

The root of the blue camas was used for food.

Page 10

Western Chokecherry
(Prunus virginiana)

The fruits were used for food. The ground seeds were preserved to flavor the pounded meat of game animals and waterfowl.

Page 11

Page 12

Yellow Pine
(Pinus ponderosa)

The inner bark was used for food. The resin was used to help treat bruises and sores. Trunks were hallowed out for boats.

Page 13

Arrowleaf/ Duck Potato/ Tule Potato/ Wapato
(Sagittaria latifolia)

The tubers of this plant were used for food.

Page 14

Narrowleaf Willow
(Salix exigua)

The wood was used for constructing nomadic dwellings and for drill points. Stems were used for rigid basketry.

Page 15

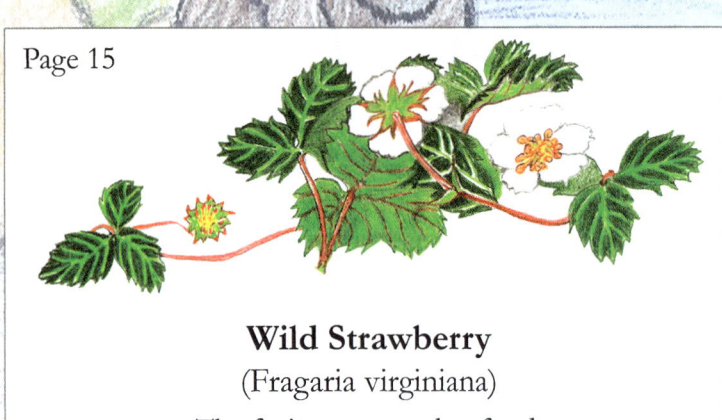

Wild Strawberry
(Fragaria virginiana)

The fruits were used as food.

Page 16

Cow Parsnip
(Heracleum lanatum)

The stems and shoots were used for food. The root was chewed or infusion was made to help with colds and coughs. Infusions were also used for headaches, root compress for the eyes, and salve was made for bruises.

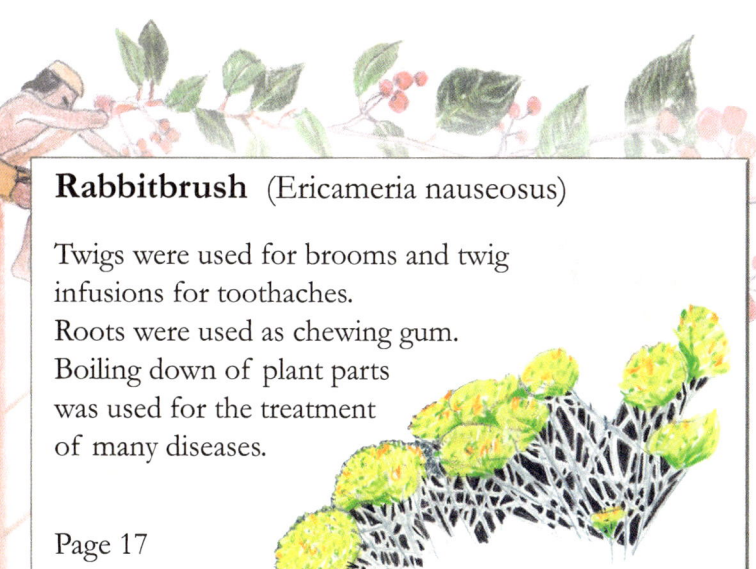

Rabbitbrush (Ericameria nauseosus)

Twigs were used for brooms and twig infusions for toothaches.
Roots were used as chewing gum.
Boiling down of plant parts was used for the treatment of many diseases.

Page 17

Yarrow
(Achillea millefolium)

Seeds were food. Whole plant infusions were used to treat infections, colds, coughs, fever, bites, and stings.
Poultice of leaves was used for wounds as it stimulates blood clotting.

Page 18

Page 19

Tule
(Schoenoplectus acutus occidentalis)

Roots, stems, and shoots were used for food. Fibers were used to make baskets, mats, clothing, cradles, quivers and rafts.

Sagebrush (Artemisia tridentata)

Fibers were used for basketry and torch material. Wood was used for fire drills. Pulp made from sagebrush was applied to aches and pains. Leaves were chewed for gastrointestinal disorders or an infusion of leaves was used for fever.

Page 20

Page 21

Yellow Pond Lily / Wokas
(Nuphar polysepalum)

The seeds of this plant were used for food.

Animal Tracker - Can you match the

tracks to the animals who made them?

Answer Key 1.D 2.I 3.N 4.B 5.L 6.F 7.J 8.E 9.M 10.H 11.P 12.A 13.O 14.G 15.Q 16.C 17.K

Author Linda Stevenson Wallace

Linda Catherine Stevenson Wallace has a passion for writing. She is a columnist, speaker, and educator. Teaching all grade levels helped expand her knowledge. She especially enjoyed teaching astronomy, history, writing, and science. Incorporating outdoor animals, trees, and track identification, using a theme approach in the classroom, contributed to the collaboration with the artist in constructing this book. She incorporated sensory awareness aspects in her classroom teaching, especially in daily writing, which is evident in this book.

As an elementary school teacher, Northern California Writers' Teacher Consultant, Keynote Speaker, and inspirational guest speaker for conferences, she enjoys entertaining many with inspiring stories, just like this one. Her weekly column, called "Second Look" for Southern Siskiyou Newspapers allows her to entertain readers, educating others on any given subject. Love and appreciating others is her greatest motto!

Linda has found it hard enduring the devastating effects of multiple sclerosis. It has helped her learn to love herself and carry on with God's unconditional love to write books, speak, and tell stories!

She is one of six children raised on a cattle ranch between Cedarville and Eagleville, California giving her material for her stories. Growing up in Surprise Valley near the borders of Oregon and Nevada provided her lessons in practical living and endurance.

Linda and her husband are parents to two sons, their wives, and two wonderful grandchildren, Zane and Lilyana Snow. Her husband is also a teacher. He is her inspiration and dearest friend. They reside in Northern California near the majestic Mount Shasta.

Illustrator Kathleen Langford

Born in Weaverville, CA, in 1948, she was raised along the Trinity River. She first lived in Big Bar with her parents and three sisters on her grandfather's homestead/mining claim. When she was nine, her family moved a few miles up the river to Junction City. From Trinity High School in Weaverville, she went to UC Berkeley where she received a BA in English and Art in 1969. In 1972, she received her elementary teaching credential from California College of Arts and Crafts (now California College of the Arts) in Oakland. Married by this time and with a first child on the way, she was happy to head back to northern California in 1974 when her husband took his first teaching assignment in Weed. This is where she has put down roots, raising four children and numerous other animals on the family's mini homestead in Hammond Ranch. She was the art teacher at Weed Elementary School for twenty years, adding Weed High School art for eleven of those years. She and her husband both retired from teaching in 2007.

For these illustrations, she called on her love of the plant world. The page borders were designed using graph paper to mimic basket patterns. The realistic part of the plant was often taken from drawings she already had in her sketch books kept over many years. Since she is part Klamath River Indian on her father's side, she felt a special kinship with the subject matter and did much research on early Native American tribes of the Mount Shasta region, especially the Modoc.

In the summer of 1857, Joaquin Miller herded horses in Now-ow-wa (near McCloud) and married Sutatot, daughter of the Wintu chief Worrotetot, meaning "short one," but was called Black Beard by the whites. Calla or Calle Shasta, their first daughter, was born around 1859. Miller left, but then mother and daughter were kidnapped by Modoc Indians. They were rescued in 1866 or '67 by Jim Brock, an old cabin-mate of Joaquin's. In 1872, Calla Shasta was sent to Oakland to attend school and live with Miller's mentor and writer, Ina Coolbrith.

Sutatot married and lived with Jim Brock in a cabin on the Pit River and was known as Amanda Brock. In Joaquin Miller's "Life Amongst the Modocs: Unwritten History," chapter 33, "The Last of the Children of Shasta," Miller describes Calle Shasta and assigns the name of Paquita to Sutatot in other novels.

—from The Californians, a magazine of California history; Jan/Feb 1992, pages 40 -44; Margaret Guilford-Kardell

"Did the world ever stop to consider how an Indian who has no theatre, no saloon, no whiskey shop, no parties, no newspaper, not one of all our hundreds of ways and means of amusement, spends his evening? Think of this!

He is a human being, full of passion and of poetry. His soul must find some expression; his heart some utterance. The long, long nights of darkness, without any lighted city to walk about in, or books to read. Think of that!

... What if I told you that they talk more of the future and know more of the unknown...

—Joaquin Miller
Life Amongst the Modocs, 1873. p.23

Made in the USA
Charleston, SC
02 October 2013